GOLDIE LOCKS
AND THE THREE
SEXY BEAR SHIFTERS

LACY JANE

LACY JANE

Goldie Locks and the Three Sexy Bear Shifters: A Steamy Reverse Harem Romance

(Once Upon a Time: Twisted Sexy Fairy Tales—Book 1)

Contents

Preface

Once upon a time, there were fairy tales. No. Not that kind. These are not fairy tales for children. These are very adult, twisted, sexy fairy tales to keep you warm at night. There will be several in this series. I hope you enjoy them.

Love,

Lacy

One

Goldie

Once upon a time, there was a girl named Goldie Locks, who had very naughty dreams...

I'm not like other girls my age. While they daydream about the captain of the football team or the cute boy in their math class, I daydream about three bear shifters. Actually, I daydream, nightdream, all the time dream, and am fucking obsessed with them.

The first time I dreamt of them, I had just turned thirteen…

There were three huge bears standing at the foot of a massive bed. They stared at me so strangely, almost like they were starving for me. It should have frightened me, but instead it made my tummy flutter.

I woke up longing to see the bears again. I have had tons of dreams about playing outside with them, laughing and feeling so happy. I have dreamt about them regularly over the years, but the dreams have happened more frequently and become much, much dirtier over the last few months.

I should introduce myself. I'm Goldie Locks. Seriously. My parents both have a really twisted sense of humor and thought it would be hilarious to name me Goldie. Now the joke is on them since I'm obsessed with three bears. Ha ha.

Since I turned eighteen last month, the dreams have become a nightly thing. They have gotten to the point that they take over the second I fall asleep. One of the dreams I have the most often, I had again last night…

I'm lying on a massive bed. The three men rush into the room in their bear forms. They stare at me as if they want to feast on me, but I know that they are not dangerous to me. They swiftly morph into the sexy men I've been dreaming about for years. Three men, so similar, yet so different.

They are all huge; at least six foot eight or nine. They have muscles upon muscles and are much broader than other men. Their hair is jet black, and their eyes are nearly black, too, with flecks of gold. They have neatly trimmed beards that I know will tickle when they kiss me. Their arms are massive, like they live in the gym, and their chests are ripped, too, with just enough hair to be sexy to the extreme. They each have that awesome vee that some men have that points down to their huge cocks. Wow. And yum. They are obviously brothers, but I can easily tell them apart despite the fact that they look so similar with their tan skin and dark hair.

I look down at their monstrous, hard cocks and feel moisture pool between my legs. They want me just as desperately as I want them. "Please," I beg them, writhing on the bed. They waste no time in ripping my clothes off of me. Instead of scaring me, their hunger just turns me on even more.

"Angel, we are your mates," the tallest of the three tells me while gently stroking my cheek. "We are going to mark you, pleasure you, and make you ours."

"Yes, please," I whisper. "Do whatever you want to me."

No sooner have I said that than the man takes my mouth in a ravenous kiss. He continues making love to my mouth while running his hands all over my body. I rub my hands up and down his chest before reaching for the hardness between his legs. It takes both of my hands to wrap around his girth. I give his cock a squeeze before working my hands down the length. Pre-cum is already spilling out, arousing me more. He pushes me down on the bed before sucking one nipple, then the other. It feels so good, but I need more. Then he puts his mouth against my pussy and devours it. He sucks on my clit, sending me spiraling. His beard is soaked with my juices. The other two get on either side of me, kissing my mouth, face, and neck before sucking my nipples and bringing my hands up to stroke both of their cocks.

So many mouths, hands, and cocks. All I feel is pleasure and the desperate need to be filled by them. I squirm under their ministrations; loving the sensations, but wanting so much more. They keep switching places so that everyone has a taste of my mouth, nipples, and pussy. Each of the men makes me come on their fingers and mouth. My screams of pleasure fill the room.

"We need to make you ours now," the sexy leader says while stroking his enormous cock.

"Yes, please!" I beg.

He moves over me and drives inside me with one hard thrust. I gasp at the sensation. It doesn't hurt as much as I had assumed it would. Instead, after a pinch of discomfort, I feel so much pleasure, it overwhelms me. With each thrust of his hips, I orgasm, soaking the bed with my cum. The others watch, waiting their turns and stroking their cocks.

"We are going to breed you tonight, sweetness," he whispers as he slams his cock into me again and again. As he lets go, he bites my nipple and pinches my clit. I scream as I orgasm again and feel him release stream after stream of cum into my hungry *pussy. I know that he is right. These three incredibly virile men are going to get me pregnant tonight, and the thought amps up my desire even more.*

He gives me a deep, passionate kiss before moving away from me. The second man takes his place. "Turn around, sweetheart. Up on all fours."

He kisses me gently before stroking my ass and pussy, working me into a frenzy with his fingers. I do as instructed and am rewarded with his cock filling me completely from behind. He pulls me against him and slams into me so hard, it almost hurts, but I want more. "Please don't hold back," I tell him. Apparently, that's all he needs to hear. He lifts me up and slams into me, again and again. As with his brother, my orgasms bleed into each other until I don't know where one ends and another begins. He holds me against him as he releases his cum inside me.

I am worn out, but I know the last man is still waiting for me, and I want him just as desperately as I wanted the other two. He motions for me to stand. I gasp as he picks me up like a rag doll and starts fucking me standing up, impaling me on his hard cock again and again until I'm running out of breath. I come continuously as he slams me down onto his cock over and over again. He releases inside me and gently lowers me to the bed. I'm surrounded by the three of them. They each reveal their sharp teeth, and lower them to my body; biting me at the same time. The ecstasy rolls through me so strongly, I pass out.

So, you see what I mean? Seriously, how is a wimpy little teenage boy going to compare to my three sexy bear shifters? Every time I dream about them, I wake up extremely horny and dripping from orgasms. All I can think about is having their hard cocks inside of me.

I've told my parents about my dreams. Well, not the specifics, but they pretty much get the gist. They are very open minded, and, frankly, don't seem as disturbed by the whole idea as you would think. That's why they are supporting my coming here today. I had a different dream last night; well, more like a flash. It showed a sign that said Landry National Park, so that's where I am now. It's a few hours from my house in Lambert, Colorado, but I feel like I'm supposed to be here. So I'm here. Hiking. Not my thing at all, but it really is beautiful here. I've seen some wild animals-deer, squirrels, and even a fox, but no bears yet. Are my shifters here? I really hope so. You have no idea how badly I want to meet and (let's be real) fuck my very sexy mates. I feel like I am getting closer to finding them.

I take a moment to appreciate the beauty surrounding me. This forest really is breathtaking. I don't think I've been anywhere so lovely before. I'm surrounded by mountains. It somehow makes me feel a sense of peace I've never felt anyplace else.

I've only been walking for a couple of hours, but I'm suddenly exhausted. I see smoke through the trees. I walk into a clearing and see the most perfect log cabin imaginable. Its wrap around porch and rocking chairs look so inviting. "It's stunning," I breathe reverently. Maybe the people inside will take pity on me, and let me lie down and take a nap. I knock on the door several times, but no one answers. "Hello?" I say, trying the doorknob. It's unlocked. I walk in and find that the cabin is even more impressive on the inside. The soaring wood ceilings are probably twenty feet tall. The cabin is almost all one massive room with a chef's kitchen, spacious living room, and the biggest bed I've ever seen. There's something vaguely familiar about it, but I'm too tired to think about what it might be. I try it out. It is the softest, most comfortable mattress I have ever felt. It feels like I'm lying on a fluffy cloud. I smile and fall immediately into a deep slumber.

Two

Jonah

Shifters sometimes dream of their mates before meeting them. This is definitely true for my brothers and me. The dreams have gone on for years now. Just glimpses of our angel at first, then full on fuck fests. The three of us have known for a long time now that we would be sharing a mate. It was a little shocking at first, but we have come to terms with it. John, Jake, and I are triplets, after all, and are way closer than most brothers. We even share a massive bed. We live together, work together, and hang out together. We are as close as any brothers could possibly be; plus we have the whole shifter thing going on.

A lot of people don't even realize that shifters are real. They think they are just something in romance novels. Surprise! We do exist. Anyway. We keep to ourselves, in general. We live in a cabin in the mountains, pretty far from everyone. We make sure to only shift into our bear forms when no one else is around. We are pretty isolated, so that's really not a problem. We are miles from the nearest neighbor. We have to be careful, though. You never know what crazy ideas someone might get about us. We have heard horror stories about shifters even being experimented on. That's why it's always a good idea to stay under the radar.

In case you don't know, there is only one fated mate for each shifter. Well, in this case, a shared mate. Anyway, that mate is the only one the shifter will ever feel desire or love for. Shifters mate for life. End of story.

We all started dreaming about our angel at the same time. The last few months, though, we have been dreaming about her nonstop. She looks very young and beautiful with her golden hair, pale skin, and baby blue eyes. I'm assuming by the incredibly curvy body she has, that she is of age now and we will be able to find her soon.

We've gone into town some, and even gone to neighboring towns as well, hoping to pick up her scent. Nothing. Damn, I really hope we find her before long. The three of us are starting to get really grumpy. It's tough seeing your mate every night in your dreams, but not being able to touch her in real life.

We are not too far from the cabin, chopping up downed trees for firewood, when an incredibly delicious scent hits us. The three of us go completely still with shock. "It's gotta be her, right?" John asks.

"I'd say so. Let's find out."

We quickly shift into our bear forms and race toward the amazing scent of our beautiful, perfect mate.

Three

Goldie

I'm dreaming again. Obviously. I look up and see the three bears. They are gigantic. A normal person would be scared to death, but not me. I live for these dreams where I see my mates. I know my bears would never hurt me. They shift into their human forms.

My lord, they are hot. "Oh my god. You are all so gorgeous," I say, looking at my very sexy mates. I am suddenly so turned on that I can't think straight. I rub my clit, which is absolutely drenched. My panties are ruined. I look up to see my three ravenous men looking like they plan to eat me for dinner.

"Angel, you are our mate," the first man growls while staring at me. His voice sends shivers down my spine. "You belong to us." The others nod in agreement.

"Yes!" I rush to agree. "I am yours. Please do whatever you want to me," I say, while fingering my pussy and lifting my hips off the bed in invitation. I hear growls from all three of them, and look up to see each of them stroking their massive cocks. I scream as an orgasm hits me hard.

Suddenly, the men are everywhere. They are dragging my shoes off, and immediately pull my pants and panties off after. They tear my shirt off, sending buttons flying, then undo my bra and throw it across the room. Damn, this dream really feels real. At least, that's what I assume until one of the men puts his mouth on my pussy and I gush all over his face.

"Oh my gosh. I'm not dreaming. Am I?" I manage to ask.

"No, sunshine. You are not dreaming. This is real. We have been dreaming about you for years now, and you are finally here. You have no idea how hungry we are for you."

"Well, then. Why don't you show me? Fuck me, mate."

Four

Jonah

Jesus. Our angel is the sexiest thing I've ever laid eyes on. I know my brothers feel the same. We have been dreaming about her for so long. I can't believe she is actually here. We rip the rest of her clothes off her sexy body. I would be worried about scaring her, but our girl is totally on board. When she came on my face, it took everything I had not to come right then. The only place I'm putting my seed is where it belongs; inside my mate's sweet cunt.

I lick her delicious honey hole again and again; fucking her with my tongue. I use my fingers to help loosen her up. She will be taking three giant bear shifters, and we aren't exactly known for being gentle; especially when we find our mate. I suck her clit hard, causing her to come again.

We each take turns kissing her pouty pink lips and licking and sucking every inch of her beautiful body. Her pale skin is the softest I've ever touched; like a baby's skin. She's short, but has incredible curves. She is perfect for fucking and breeding. She looks like a sexy centerfold with her long blond hair spread out behind her, and her bare pussy glistening. Her heavy tits are the most incredible things I've ever seen. I take my time sucking and biting her rosy little nipples, while my brothers take turns licking her honey pot.

She is writhing on the bed, primed and ready for us. Her vanilla scent mixed with her arousal is driving me insane.

"Open up, sweetness. It's time to fuck your mates."

Five

Goldie

<hr>

"Yes!" I scream. I've never needed anything so badly in my entire life. My pussy feels so empty. It longs to be rammed with the gigantic hard cocks my mates are sporting. I spread my legs eagerly; ready to be filled.

The first man lines his cock up to my drenched hole and slams himself inside. I scream, both with a stab of pain and the most pleasure I've ever experienced. My fingernails are probably drawing blood as they dig into his back. He gives me a few seconds to get used to his size before he pulls back and slams in again. He does this a few times until I have every bit of his giant cock inside of me. I can hear his ragged breathing, along with that of my other mates.

"I'll try to be gentle, little one, but it's not going to be easy for me." I look into his beautiful eyes and inhale his manly scent. These men all smell amazing; like leather, outdoors, and men. Big, strong, burly, sexy men.

"Please don't be gentle," I say breathlessly. "I need to be taken hard by all three of you."

The men groan in unison before the man starts pounding into my pussy so hard that the headboard is slamming against the wall. Orgasm after orgasm burst from me so strong that I'm afraid I might pass out. He lifts my legs over his arms and pounds into me even deeper.

"You love me fucking the hell out of your sweet little cunt, don't you, Angel?"

"Yes!" I scream as another orgasm wracks my body.

"We're going to breed you!" he screams as he presses his finger against my clit hard, making me come again.

"Yes!" I scream, raking my nails down his back as I take rope after rope of his seed inside my greedy cunt.

Six

Jake

"My turn," I growl, practically knocking Jonah out of the way. Our girl has just been thoroughly fucked, but I can't give her time to recover. I've waited thirty-five years to find my mate. I could have eaten her sweet pussy all day long. I'm already addicted to the taste and scent of her. I'm not about to wait another second to be inside her.

"On your hands and knees, baby." I kiss her lips and neck before flipping her over and slamming myself to the hilt inside her warm, wet hole. "Fuck!" I yell. "Your sweet little pussy is choking the life out of my cock."

Damn. The wetness dripping from her tells me she likes it when I talk nasty. "You like me talking dirty to you?" I ask as I pump into her harder.

"Yes," she answers breathlessly.

"Damn, that's hot. Beg me to fuck you, baby."

"Please fuck me harder! I need your cock!"

I rare back and plow into her with everything I've got. I pinch her hard little nipples while I fuck her. My brother is right. We are definitely getting our girl pregnant tonight. Just the thought of her belly round with our baby sends me over the edge, making me spill my load inside her beautiful body.

Seven

John

"I need you, too," our angel says once my brother finishes with her.

"About fucking time," I growl, picking her up and impaling her on my giant cock in one move, making her scream. I groan. She feels even better than I had imagined. "Jesus. You feel incredible. I'm sorry to be so rough with you, angel. I just want you too much to go slow."

"Don't worry. I don't want you to go slow. I like it hard and rough."

Damn. She is perfect. I fuck her even harder. Her hot little cunt is squeezing the hell out of my cock. Every time she comes, her pussy squeezes me tighter. I pound into her like my very own fuck toy, and she loves every minute of it. I've never heard sexier sounds in my life than the cries and screams our girl makes while she's being fucked by one of us.

I hold out as long as possible, but our sexy girl is too much. Watching her ripe tits bounce in front of my face as I fuck her tests my control. Before long, her tight as hell pussy finally milks all the cum from my body.

I roll off of her and give her a few minutes to rest and recoup. I look at my brothers, who both nod at me. We have to explain what's about to happen. "We all have to bite you at the same time to finish the mating ritual, sweetheart," I say gently, while stroking her cheek. The three of us are nervous about her reaction. Most humans freak out when they hear something like that, but not our angel. She is perfect for us in every way.

"I know," she says calmly. "Finish making me yours."

We take turns kissing her hungrily, before piercing her skin with our sharp teeth. The pleasure is so intense, the four of us orgasm hard and pass out.

Eight

Goldie

"Best. Dream. Ever," I mumble as I start to wake up. When I try to roll over, though, I find I can't move. As I shift my legs, the ache between them tells me that last night really happened. I open my eyes and see all three of my mates in bed with me, in all their naked glory. Finally! Instead of waking up alone and horny, I am waking up with the three hottest men I've ever seen. Definitely still horny, though. I think they can help me with that. Damn, but my mates are fine! I rake my eyes down their sexy, naked bodies. Every inch of them makes me hot. No wonder no one else has ever interested me. No one else could possibly compare.

The three of them wake at once, and stare hungrily at me. As sore as it is, my pussy aches, wanting more of the three men. They start stroking their hands up and down my body; my arms, my legs, my breasts. I ache everywhere. I am shocked to see their cocks completely hard again. "Oh, my," I breathe, excited to see what else they have in store for me. They take turns kissing me for several minutes before stopping to talk to me.

Nine

Jonah

As much as I want our angel again, I know we should at least spend some time getting to know her first. We need to treat our mate with love and respect, but it's really tough when your dick is doing all the thinking for you.

"Sweetheart, before we take you again, we should probably introduce ourselves. I'm Jonah Bear. These are my brothers, Jake and John."

"Hi. I'm Goldie. Goldie Locks."

We all burst out laughing. "Seriously, sweetheart. What's your name?"

"I promise you, Jonah, I am not even kidding. That is actually my name."

He smiles. "I suppose it's pretty appropriate, considering."

She smiles and nods. "Is Bear seriously your last name?"

"Yes, baby. It is. And it will be added to your name as soon as possible."

"That sounds wonderful, but I think I need to spend a little more time in bed with my mates first. Don't you? I have an ache right here," I say, dipping my fingers in my dripping wet cunt. "You three are the only ones who can make it better."

We all growl and jump on our gorgeous mate. We'll have to leave this cabin at some point, but it definitely won't be today. I push her down and have my mouth on her cunt before she knows what hit her. Damn, I could lick her honey all day long, but my cock needs his turn, too. I pull her on top of me and watch her impale herself on my dick.

"Fuck!" we both cry at the same time. Watching her fuck me is so sexy. Her sweet pussy is squeezing my cock like a vise. Her heavy tits bounce in front of my face. I squeeze them hard, then take turns sucking and biting her hard nipples. She really likes it when I'm a little rough with them. She looks like a goddess as she rides me. She starts rocking faster until I finally have to take over. I lay her down on the bed, put her legs over my arms and pound the hell out of her sweet cunt. She screams out as she comes again and milks my release out of me.

Ten

Jake

"Brother, you gotta share," I say as gently as I can. Jonah gives Goldie a sweet kiss, then rolls off to the other side of the bed to recover. My mate is laid out before me like the finest feast, and I can't wait to sample everything on the menu.

"Come here, sweetheart," I motion for her to come to the edge of the bed. "I need to feel your sweet mouth wrapped around my cock." She licks her puffy lips hungrily, then devours half of my cock on the first try.

"Damn, baby. That feels so good." She gags a little as she tries to take too much. "You don't need to take it all, sweetness. We'll love anything you do to us."

She pulls back and starts licking the head of my cock like a lollipop. She scoops out some pre-cum with her tongue and swallows it. "Mmmm. Delicious."

I need to come, but every bit is going inside of her ripe pussy. I toss her on the bed and fuck her like the animal I am. I have no control when it comes to her. I can't get enough. I slam my cock inside her again and again, loving the noises she makes and the cum that drips from her sweet little hole. The sound of my cock going in and out of her is loud in the quiet room. She screams out and her cunt grips my cock so hard, I can't hold out any longer. I come so hard, I black out.

Eleven

John

"Come here, sweetheart. Ride my cock."

Goldie smiles as she lowers herself onto my throbbing dick. Damn. She feels so good. It takes everything I have not to come immediately. Her warm heat grips me as she slams herself down on my cock, harder and harder.

"Help me," she says. I know what she needs. Our girl likes it really hard. I grip her shoulders, pushing her down even harder, until I feel her cervix against my dick.

"Yes!" she screams. I slam her down on my cock faster and faster, loving the feel of liquid gushing from her. Finally, I let go and come hard in her sweet, addictive pussy.

Twelve

Goldie

After spending a glorious morning in bed, we decide to go outside into the beautiful forest. My mates introduce me to their bears. They are three giant grizzlies, who look terrifying, but are total teddy bears with me. They vie for my attention like little children. Each pushes their head against my hand, wanting to be petted like a dog. They take turns licking my face, sending me into a fit of giggles. After that, they let me ride on their backs while they run around. I feel so free and happy with my mates.

They cook me a delicious dinner of steak and vegetables. I sit and watch them preparing the meal since they won't let me do anything. They treat me like a queen.

I have learned so much about them today. They sell firewood and make custom wood furniture. It's all very impressive. They even built their gorgeous cabin themselves.

They only go into town once a month or so for supplies. They have a massive extra refrigerator and freezer in the garage so that they have plenty of food in case of a snowstorm. They have a backup generator, too. They are pretty self sufficient, for the most part. There's enough food here to sustain them for several months.

After dinner, we spend the rest of the evening outside running around again before finally collapsing. Today has been filled with lots of sex and getting to know each other. We are all exhausted. We need to get a good night's sleep tonight, though. After all, tomorrow is a big day. I am taking my mates to meet my parents.

Thirteen

John

Today, we are on our way to meet Goldie's parents. She's our mate no matter what, but it would be nice if her parents could like and accept us.

She looks over at me. "Don't look so worried. My parents have known for years that I would be mated to the three of you. I know it sounds nuts, but they are very accepting. They just want me to be happy."

"That's what we want, too, baby."

"The three of you make me very happy."

I pull her into my lap for a kiss. But the longer I kiss her, the more I want. So does she. Before I know it, she is grinding her sweet little pussy against me, and I can't hold back anymore. Her dress provides easy access. I push it up, rip the soaked panties from her body, and release my steel rod from the denim prison he is in. There's no time for finesse. I lay her down on the backseat and push all the way inside her drenched cunt. I nearly come just from hearing her moans of pleasure.

"What the fuck?" Jonah says.

"Hey, man! This has to be equal," Jake chimes in.

"Brother, you are so right," Jonah slaps him on the shoulder, and turns off of the highway.

We pull onto a dirt road, but I couldn't care less. I'm fucking my woman so hard I'm seeing stars. I finally come inside her and collapse. After a few seconds, I am lifted off of her.

"My turn," growls Jonah.

Fourteen

Jonah

It took everything I had to not pull over and fuck Goldie before, but when John started screwing her, there was no way in hell I was waiting any longer. She looks at me and smiles. I kiss her soft lips and squeeze her juicy tits. I can't wait to see them filled with milk. Just the thought of it makes me even harder. "I can't take it slow, Goldie."

"Good. I don't want you to. Fuck me as hard as you want, Jonah."

I shed my clothes and plow inside her sweet cunt. "Fuck, sweet pea. I could do this all day."

"Me, too," she moans. I devour her mouth and tits while I fuck her, never letting up. Her cries get louder and louder.

"You love it when I fuck you hard, don't you?" I breathe against her ear.

"Yes! I love it! I love when you fuck me. I love all three of you."

That's enough to milk every drop of cum from my body. I pull her against me; raining kisses on her face and giving her a minute to rest before Jake takes over.

Fifteen

Jake

It's my turn to have our sweet mate. We aren't going to make it to her parents' house today because we had to have her again. I punch my hips forward and pound her sweet, sweet pussy. She nips my ear and bites my neck, sending me into overdrive.

"You're my dirty little girl, aren't you?"

"Yes, I'm your dirty girl. Fuck me hard, Jake."

"You love your mates' giant cocks, don't you?"

"Yes!" she screams, while I pound her pussy mercilessly. "Put your baby in me." Her sexy words are enough to push me over the edge.

Darkness consumes me as I fall into the deepest sleep of my life.

Sixteen

Goldie

We all ended up sleeping in the truck last night. You would think it would be horribly uncomfortable, but it really wasn't. Even though my men are ridiculously muscular, they are really comfy to sleep on. Not to mention, we were all really worn out.

I had let my mom know we would be coming by today. She didn't sound too surprised. She had assumed I would find my mates. I just hope everything goes well.

"It will be fine," Jonah whispers in my ear.

"Are you a mind reader?"

"Just with you. Now that we are mated, we can read each other's thoughts."

"Seriously? Huh. I didn't know that."

"There's a lot you don't know, but we will teach you."

"I'd really like that," I say, giving his hand a squeeze.

Seventeen

Jonah

"See. What did I tell you?" I say to her mentally.

"This is so weird," she sends back.

Joe and Beth Locks, Goldie's parents, are as nice as they can be. Beth looks like an older, tinier version of our beautiful mate, while Joe is tall with salt and pepper hair and our angel's blinding smile. I really expected judgment or anger from the two of them, but all they show us is love and acceptance. They know a few mated couples, so they know how it works; although our situation is a bit different. I can feel the relief flowing from Goldie that everything is going so well. I ask for their permission to marry their daughter. Even though technically she will be married to me, in reality, she will be married to the three of us. It's very important to all of us. My brothers and I want our mate tied to us in every way, so we need to marry her as soon as possible. Her parents give us their blessing, and we all have a nice dinner to celebrate.

My brothers and I would like to marry Goldie today, but we know this is the one and only wedding for us and our angel. We finally agree that we will wait a week so that she can have everything she wants for her wedding day. We would do anything to make Goldie happy.

Eighteen

Goldie

A week later…

It's my wedding day. We are having a very private ceremony. Just me and my mates, my parents, and my soon to be in-laws, who are really wonderful. I got to meet them a few days ago. I was so nervous, but they are awesome. I love them and they love me. They aren't weirded out by our situation, thank god. They seem very excited about the possibility of having grandkids sometime soon.

Mom and I have rushed around all week, gotten everything together for the wedding, and even found the perfect dress. It's a gorgeous, strapless gown with little jewels all over it. The stones form what look like little bear paws. I kid you not. When I saw it, I knew it was the perfect dress to marry my bear shifters in.

The Wedding March starts playing, and I take my father's arm. He walks me down the aisle to my three sexy mates. Their eyes are filled with happiness and hunger, much like mine probably are. I say my vows to each of them and them to me. They place a stunning diamond on my finger, with a matching wedding band. I put a ring on each of them. I am so thankful I wore waterproof makeup as I feel tears of happiness run down my face. We are finally pronounced men and wife. We now belong to each other in every way. Each man kisses me tenderly.

"I love you all so much."

"We love you, too," they each say. They each start telling me mentally all the things they plan to do to me tonight, making me blush and drench my panties. I shift my legs, trying and failing to get some relief. I can't wait to get back to the cabin with them.

Nineteen

Goldie

We make it back home in record time. When we walk inside, I am stunned. My husbands have managed to decorate the cabin with fairy lights everywhere. It looks beautiful. The whole room glows, illuminating the many flowers adorning every surface; including the rose petals decorating the bed.

"Oh, my gosh. This is gorgeous! You guys are so good to me," I say as I hug each of my men.

"We love our beautiful mate. We just want you to be happy," Jonah says, smiling. The others nod their heads in agreement.

"I've never been so happy before," I tell them while strolling casually to the bed. "You could make me even happier, though. You know, our marriage hasn't been consummated yet." That's all it takes for my three men to surround me, kissing my lips and neck, while trying to undo all of the tiny buttons on my dress. Their giant fingers are having difficulty performing that task. I can feel desire rolling off of them. Their arousal makes mine burn that much hotter.

"Just rip it," I say heatedly. Jake rips my dress down the back. The next thing I know, my men are devouring me from head to toe. "Should we try something new?" I ask them.

"Like what?" John asks.

"Taking all three of you at once?" They each growl and their cocks seem to get even harder.

"Are you sure about this, sweetheart?" Jonah asks.

"Yes. I want every part of me to belong to the three of you."

Each of the men strip quickly. They silently agree on positions. Jonah lies down on the bed, pulling me on top of him. It only takes me a couple of tries to get his cock all the way inside of my hungry pussy. Jake gets behind me, sliding one finger, then two into my puckered hole. It feels strange, but arousing. Soon, he starts pushing inside me with the head of his cock. "Oh my god!" I scream with pleasure. He manages to push all the way in.

"Me, too, angel," John says, while pushing his angry looking cock into my mouth. I take him deeper and deeper, trying not to gag. I swallow and feel his cock hitting the back of my throat. The three of them pump into me at the same time, drawing orgasm after orgasm out of my well used body. Their grunts are such a turn on. Before long, they all lose control, fucking me harder and harder until they explode inside me, triggering an intense orgasm that makes me quiver from head to toe.

"Wow," I say breathlessly.

"Wow is right," my three men say simultaneously.

"Are you okay?" Jonah asks.

"Never better," I reply, giving each of my men a passionate kiss. Jonah picks me up and carries me into the enormous shower. They take turns washing me off as I wash them. After a while, we dry off and crash for the night. Our wedding day has been perfect.

Twenty

Epilogue 1–Jonah

A month later...

I walk inside the cabin and find my wife bawling. "What's wrong, baby? What happened?"

She tries to tell me, but she's crying so hard, she doesn't make any sense. "Wedonthaveanyicecream."

"Huh? Sweetheart. Calm down for a second. Concentrate and tell me with your mind."

"We don't have any mint chocolate chip ice cream!" she screams in my head.

"It's okay, baby. We'll get you some." I call John and have him make an emergency trip to the grocery store. I don't know why this is so urgent, but I've never seen Goldie so upset. I wrap my arms around her and rock her from side to side until she calms down.

****

A short while late, John and Jake rush in with a year's supply of ice cream. Believe me, the three of us spoil the shit out of our mate every chance we get. She spies the ice cream and practically knocks us down to get to it. She grabs a spoon and scarfs down one of the pints in record time.

The three of us exchange worried glances. "Do you think she has a tapeworm?" Jake whispers. I shake my head. I'm not sure what is wrong with our mate, but she is all out of sorts.

"Thank you!" she says as she gives us each an extra long hug and kiss. Her arousal fills my nose and turns my dick to stone. "Mmm. You all smell so good," she says, while stroking our chests. "I need to feel you. Now," she says, stripping off her dress to reveal her perfect, naked body underneath. The three of us growl and waste no time shucking our clothes and satisfying our mate's craving for our cocks.
****

Later, I'm wrapped around Goldie, squeezing her luscious tits. "Damn, you are so sensitive, baby." She has come twice just from me pinching her nipples. It finally dawns on me. I sniff her cunt like the animal I am.

"What are you doing, Jonah?" she giggles.

"I'm smelling your sweet cunt that smells even sweeter than normal. You're pregnant, angel."

"What?" the three of them shout at once.

"Of course!" Jake and John agree, but our mate just looks confused.

"Sweetheart, think about it. You've been fucked countless times by three very virile shifters with no protection. You've been emotional. You've cried at several commercials. You thought the world was coming to an end when you didn't have ice cream. Your tits are super sensitive. Baby, you've got a shifter cub growing inside you."

I see the moment realization hits her. "Oh my God!" she touches her stomach reverently. "We're having a baby!" Tears of happiness stream down her face. She hugs each of us before we claim her again like the ravenous beasts we are.

Twenty-One

Epilogue 2-Goldie

Five years later…

I hear giggles as my three little bear cubs play hide and seek with their fathers. That's right. Just like my husbands, my babies are nearly identical triplets-Jackson, Jagger, and Julian. My hubbies wanted to stick with the J names. I had a really rough delivery with three giant shifter babies, so we decided to stop at three.

My parents are visiting for the weekend. I am so excited because I know I will get some quality alone time with my men tonight, because my parents are always happy to spend extra time with their grandbabies. They are awesome that way. Even after five years, I can't wait to be alone with my sexy mates. We still want each other just as much as that first time. I guess that's what happens when you are mated to three sexy shifters. Lucky me!

Our babies just started shifting recently, and it is just freaking adorable. I watch as my parents try to hold in their laughter at them. They are hiding behind a pole that is about three inches wide. They don't yet get that we can still see them. My three big bears find them and hold them down, tickling them. Their laughter echoes through the mountain. My heart is overflowing. The six of them are my everything.

Goldie Locks, the three bear shifters, and their three baby bears lived happily ever after.

THE END

If you enjoyed this book, please take a few moments to write a review of it. Thank you!

More Twisted Sexy Fairy Tales are coming soon!

Twenty-Two

Preview: Chapter 1—Scarlett and the Big, Bad, Sexy Wolf

Scarlett

Once upon a time, there was a girl named Scarlett. She was on her way to her grandma's house, not knowing that she was about to meet a big, bad, sexy wolf.

I am driving up the steep mountain road to meet Granny's realtor at her house. Granny took a vacation to Miami last month and loved it so much, she decided to move there. She came home, packed everything up, and was on her way. Which brings me to now. She asked me to show her house to Mr. Wolf, the realtor she randomly chose. After everything Granny has done for me, it's really the least that I can do. Considering she raised me as her own after my folks took off for parts unknown right after I was born, I kind of owe her. She is pretty much the only parent I have had for all of my twenty-two years. Granny is my favorite person in the world. I miss her already. I don't mind helping her out; really, I don't. My Mini Cooper just wasn't made for these mountain roads.

When I finally make it to Granny's cabin, I see that someone is already there, waiting on the front porch. I get out of my car, but when the man turns around to face me, I freeze. He is a behemoth of a man; well over six feet tall. He has sun kissed skin with short black hair, and a sexy beard I'd love to run my fingers through . He is wearing a suit that surely had to be custom made to fit his massive shoulders and chest. His eyes are a really odd amber color. They almost look like they are glowing.

The man is drop dead gorgeous, but it's not just that. I have never had any kind of attraction to anyone before, but this man is doing it for me in spades. I take a few steps toward him, and he makes an odd noise. Did he just growl at me?

Moisture pools between my legs. Damn. That has seriously never happened to me before. He takes a whiff of the air and suddenly looks ravenous. There is no way that he can know I'm wet. Right? I try to discreetly rub my legs together to get some relief, but it doesn't seem to help the ache any. I attempt to regain my composure, and approach him with an outstretched hand. "Hi. I'm Scarlett Jones, Daisy's granddaughter," I manage to squeak out.

He licks his lips. "I'm Damian Wolf," he says in his very husky voice. "Everyone just calls me Wolf, but you should call me Damian," he says, running his fingers down my neck, giving me goosebumps all over, and making my panties spontaneously combust. "I guess that makes you little red, and me, the big, bad wolf." He stares at me for so long, I feel like I'm in a trance. Instead of shaking my hand, he lifts it to his lips for a kiss. Shock waves roll through me and set every nerve in my body on fire. He spreads kisses across the top of my hand, shooting desire through my system and making me breathless. Keeping hold of my hand, he puts his mouth against my ear, making it seem very warm outside despite the dropping temperature. "You might not realize it yet, but sweetheart? You. Are. Mine."

I don't think I can say no to this man. I don't even want to. I am so fucked.

Coming October 15th!

About the Author

Lacy Jane is an empty nester and dog mom who believes in happily ever afters and has always wanted to write steamy romances. She enjoys reading, streaming shows, doing wordle, playing games, and hanging out with her hubby, kids, dogs, friends, and family. She loves to travel, shop, and drink delicious coffee drinks. She has a beauty product addiction and spends way too much time and money in Sephora and Ulta. Her books are for those who like their happily ever after a little on the dirty side. Always a steamy read with HEA guaranteed.

You can connect with me on:

- http://lacy-jane.mailchimpsites.com
- http://www.amazon.com/author/lacyjane

Subscribe to my newsletter:

✉ http://lacy-jane.mailchimpsites.com

Always a steamy read with HEA guaranteed.

Little Red and the Big, Bad, Sexy Wolf (Once Upon a Time: Twisted Sexy Fairy Tales Book 2)
When shifter Damian Wolf meets Scarlett, he'll stop at nothing, including using their uncontrollable attraction to each other, to make her his. Will the big, bad, sexy wolf and his human fated mate get their happily ever after? Find out in this modern, sexy take on Little Red Riding Hood.

This very adult fairy tale is hot, hot, hot! If you prefer your romances sweet and squeaky clean, this is not the book for you. On the other hand, if you like racy, steamy romances with sexy heroes and strong heroines, this is right up your alley.

This is the second book in my series Once Upon a Time: Twisted Sexy Fairy Tales. Each book is a stand alone, though characters from the other stories occasionally make appearances. As always, this book has high heat, no cheating, instalove, and (of course!) a HEA.

My books are for those who like their happily ever after a little on the dirty side. A steamy read with HEA guaranteed. Enjoy!

Enticing Ella (Once Upon a Time: Twisted Sexy Fairy Tales Book 3)

After a night of passion with Prince, Ella disappears. Now that he has claimed her, Prince will stop at nothing to find Ella and make her his bride. Can he save her from her evil stepmother in time? Find out in this sweet, spicy, modern version of Cinderella, complete with a ball, one evil stepmother, a fairy godmother of sorts, and Ella's adorable little dog, Cujo.

As with all of my books, this OTT romance contains high heat, instalove, no cheating, and (of course!) a HEA. My books are always a steamy read with HEA guaranteed. Enjoy!

Seduced by the Witness (Obsessed Alphas Book 1)
When a sexy FBI agent and a curvy, gorgeous witness are thrown together, sparks fly. Can they resist each other, or will they give in to their desires? Find out in this steamy, close proximity romance.

This book has instalove, high heat, no cheating, and (of course!) a HEA. My books are for those who like their happily ever after a little on the dirty side. Always a steamy read with HEA guaranteed. Enjoy!

Seducing My Wife

Can Jace convince Chloe to give him a second chance? Find out if this very passionate couple can resolve their differences in this quick, steamy read.

This book has instalove, high heat, no cheating, and (of course!) a HEA. My books are for those who like their happily ever after a little on the dirty side. Always a steamy read with HEA guaranteed. Enjoy!

Seducing Her Stalker

Can a stalker find happiness with the object of his obsession?

From the moment Jaxon sees Serena, he becomes completely obsessed with her. His life suddenly revolves around the sweet, sexy librarian. He finds himself crossing more and more lines as his obsession intensifies. When he finds out she returns his feelings, he is determined to make her his. Will she still feel the same if she finds out how deep his obsession with her is?

Like all of my books, this is an OTT instalove with high heat, no cheating, and (of course!) a HEA. If you are looking for a squeaky clean romance, I am not your girl. If you like your romance a little on the dirty side, read away! Always a steamy read with HEA guaranteed. Enjoy!